TOST LUCK BOX

Moonfeld Chronicles Book 2

By Mister Moonfeld
Illustrations by Natalya Efremova

Mister Moonfeld's Lost Luck Box

First Edition (PD092925)

Copyright © 2024 by Empowered On Media, LLC
Lake Mary, Florida, USA
All rights reserved.

Published in the United States of America by
EMPOWERED ON BOOKS
An imprint of Empowered On Media, LLC
empoweredon.com

Mister Moonfeld's™ is a trademark of Empowered On Media, LLC

ISBN: 979-8-9898346-2-4 (Paperback)
ISBN: 979-8-9898346-3-1 (Hardcover)
Library of Congress Control Number: 2024937908

Greetings!

If you are already familiar with these Chronicles, feel free to skip ahead. For those joining us for the first time, it is my pleasure to extend a warm welcome to you.

I am Mister Moonfeld, the magical groundskeeper of Turtle Island Elementary, or Mystic Horticulturist, if you prefer. My typical duties include beautifying the school grounds with plants from this world and beyond.

Since childhood, I have been captivated by the mysteries of magic. My very first successful trick was keeping my beloved dog, Sunny, forever a puppy.

Our dear principal, Grace Sensible, has tasked me with helping students navigate their most peculiar problems.

Thank you for joining me on these adventures.

With love and light,

Mister Moonfeld

Whenever Billy walked through the school, students scattered out of his way. Bad luck loomed over him like a dark cloud. He kept his hands buried in his pockets, knowing that one wrong move would trigger a chain reaction of clanks, crashes, bangs, and booms.

"Mister Moonfeld will help you," the principal said, ringing the magical groundskeeper's bell. "He's a very kind, down-to-earth person."

"He's up there," Billy said, pointing with his nose.

"You helped me regain my sense of wonder," the principal said to Mister Moonfeld. "Now, I wonder if you can help Billy recover his luck."

"He looks like a boy with a normal level of luck," Mister Moonfeld said.

"No, it's true," Billy said, forcing a smile. "My luck is gone."

The principal leaned toward Mister Moonfeld. "I'm placing this student under your supervision. A student's safety is our top priority. Is that clear?"

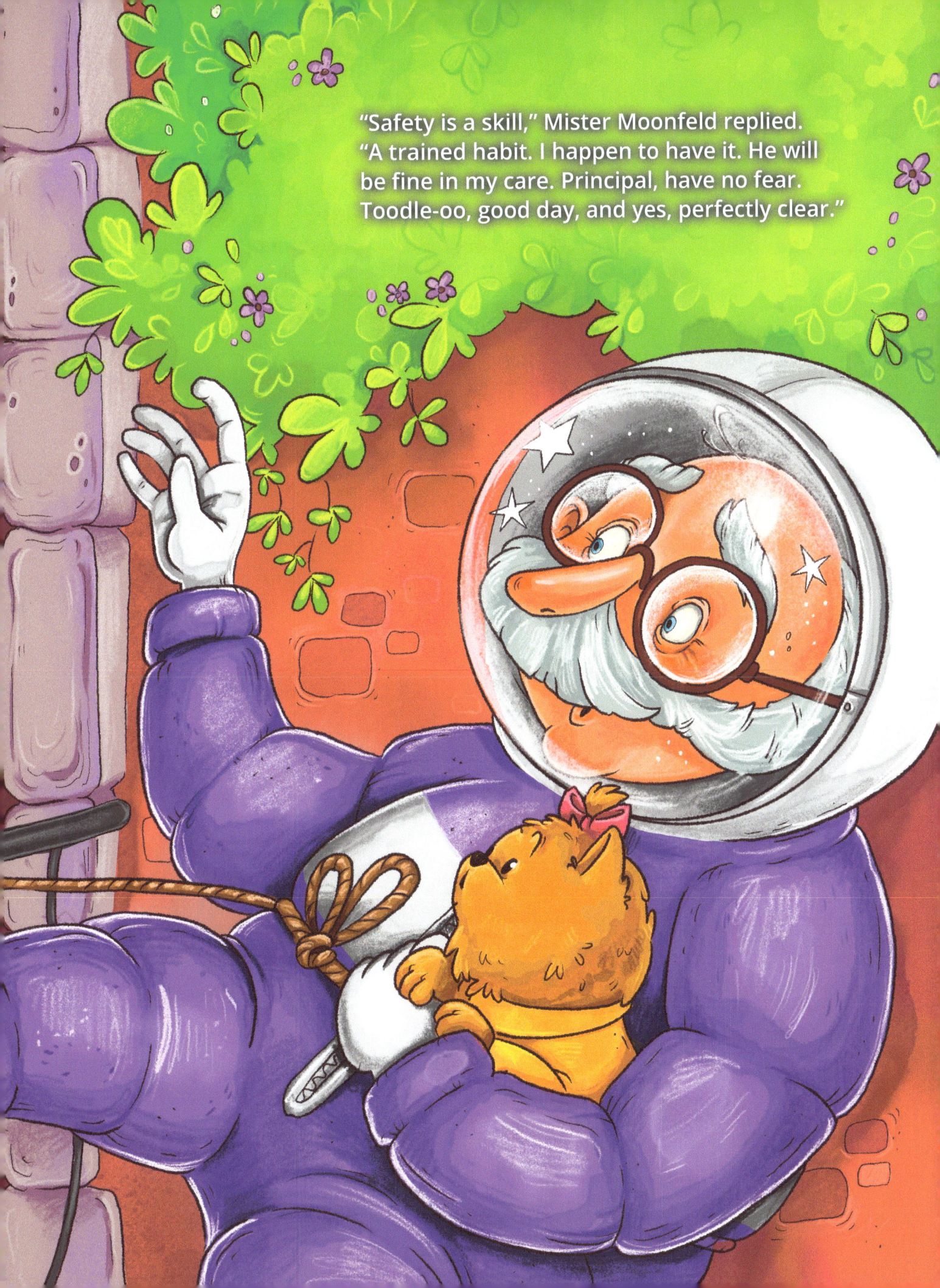

"Safety is a skill," Mister Moonfeld replied.
"A trained habit. I happen to have it. He will
be fine in my care. Principal, have no fear.
Toodle-oo, good day, and yes, perfectly clear."

The air inside Mister Moonfeld's office was still.

"Take your hands out of your pockets," Mister Moonfeld said.

Billy hesitated, his shoulders tensing. "That's not a smart idea. I'll accidentally hit one small thing, which will cause a chain reaction that breaks everything here."

"An improbable possibility, Billy. Watch this!" Mister Moonfeld danced around the room with his puppy. "You will not, no, cannot break everything in my office."

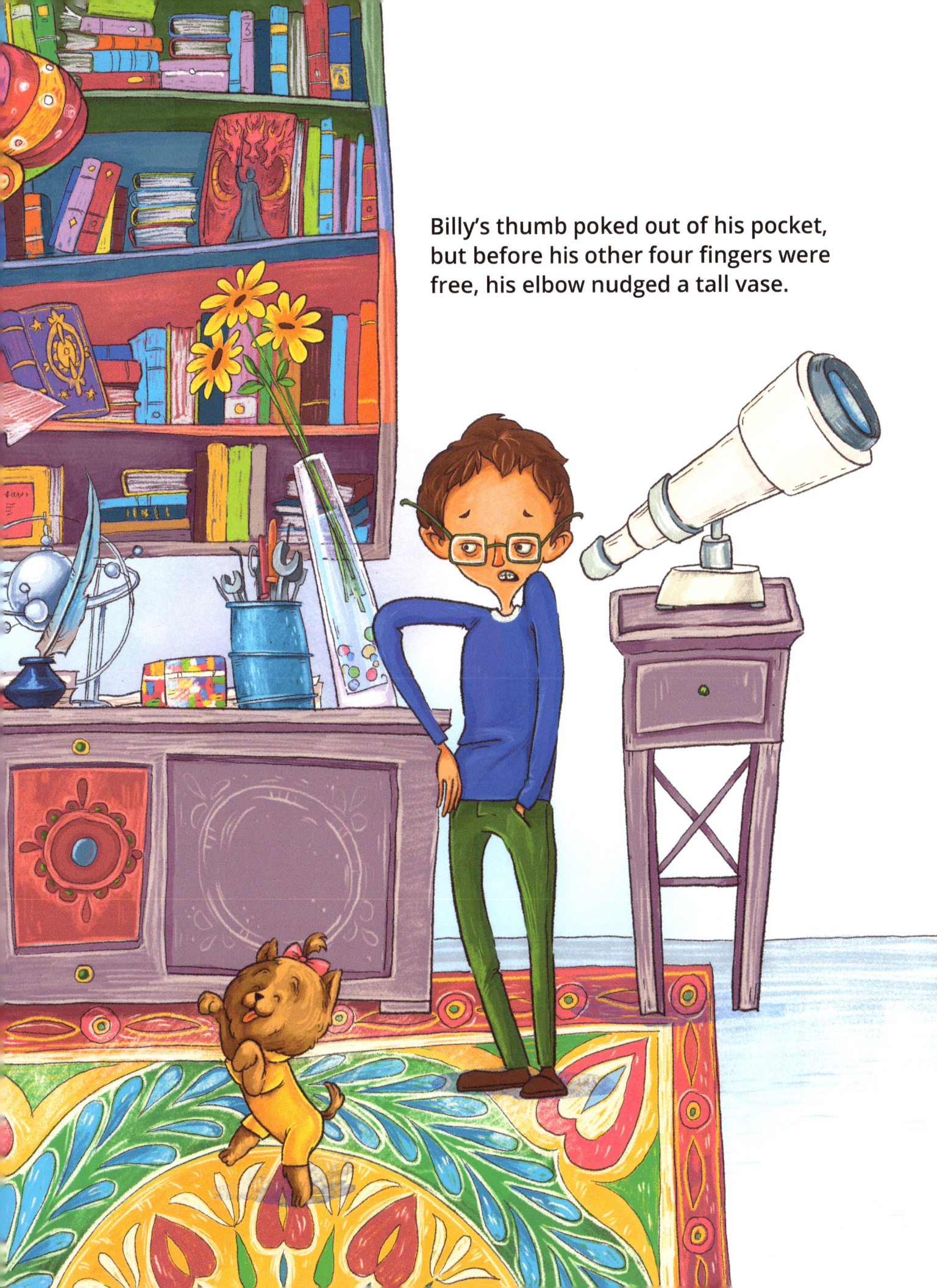

Billy's thumb poked out of his pocket, but before his other four fingers were free, his elbow nudged a tall vase.

Mister Moonfeld clutched his fish tank as everything else in the room fell apart. "See, Billy, the fish tank remains intact," he said, examining it. "Well, except for a tiny chip in a shell." He cleared his throat. "Let us imagine for a moment that you have run out of luck. Where could it have gone?"

With not much left to break nearby, Billy pointed and said, "It's locked in a box at the bottom of the sea."

Mister Moonfeld's voice filled with adventure. "Then we must journey to the depths of the sea to reclaim your treasure!"

Mister Moonfeld pulled shimmering confetti from his pocket.
"Hold tight," he said, tossing it into the air.

Sparkles flashed in Billy's eyes. When his vision cleared, he
saw that they were standing at the edge of the fish tank.
A submarine surfaced from the water.

Mister Moonfeld climbed into the submarine. "I find the waves of the sea so serene. Please pass me Sunny."

Puzzled by the mechanics of magic, Billy carefully handed over the puppy. For the briefest moment, he forgot his bad luck.

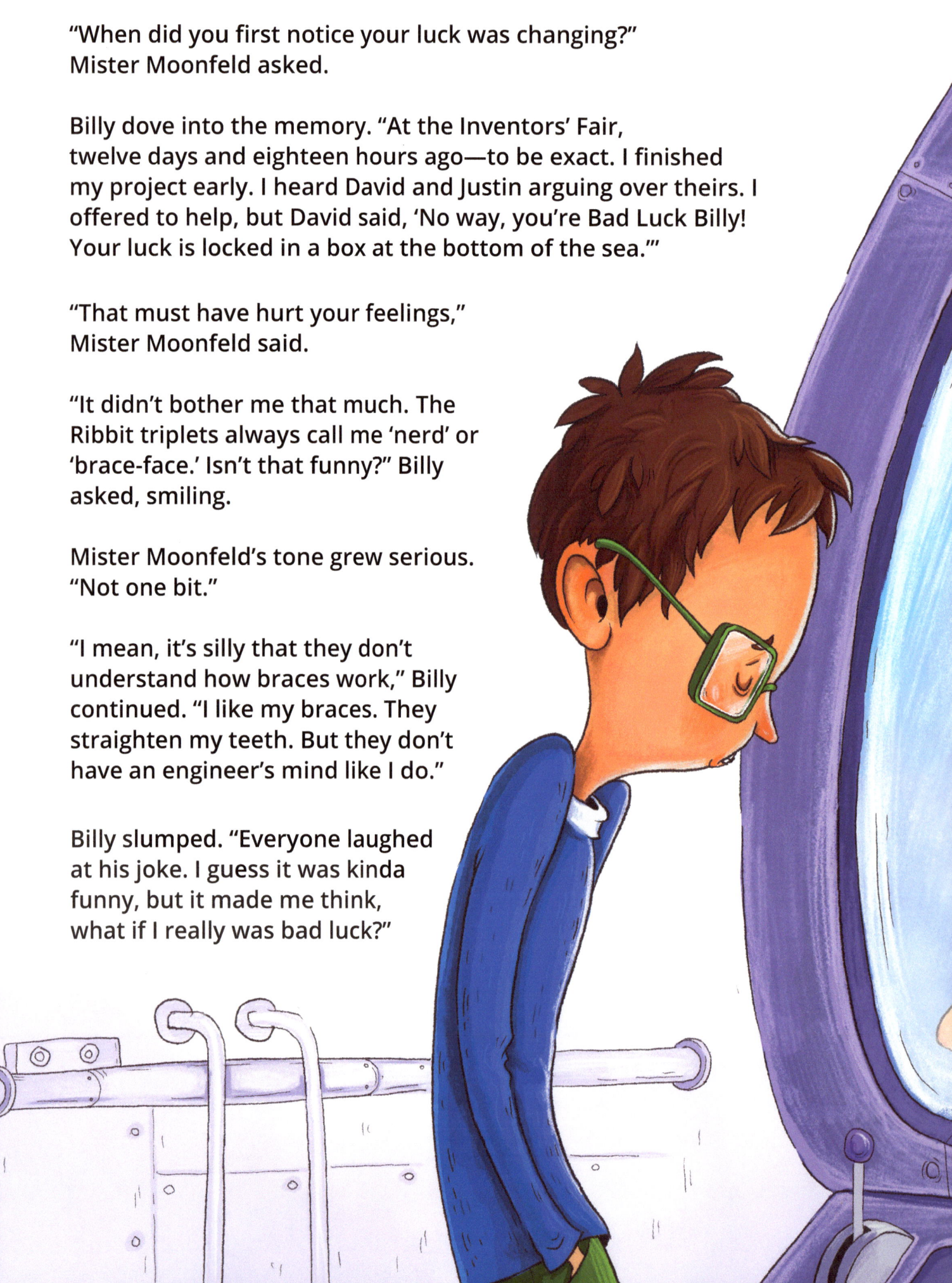

"When did you first notice your luck was changing?" Mister Moonfeld asked.

Billy dove into the memory. "At the Inventors' Fair, twelve days and eighteen hours ago—to be exact. I finished my project early. I heard David and Justin arguing over theirs. I offered to help, but David said, 'No way, you're Bad Luck Billy! Your luck is locked in a box at the bottom of the sea.'"

"That must have hurt your feelings," Mister Moonfeld said.

"It didn't bother me that much. The Ribbit triplets always call me 'nerd' or 'brace-face.' Isn't that funny?" Billy asked, smiling.

Mister Moonfeld's tone grew serious. "Not one bit."

"I mean, it's silly that they don't understand how braces work," Billy continued. "I like my braces. They straighten my teeth. But they don't have an engineer's mind like I do."

Billy slumped. "Everyone laughed at his joke. I guess it was kinda funny, but it made me think, what if I really was bad luck?"

Billy clenched his fist. He could almost feel the gear from his project pressing against his fingers, as if he were back at the Fair.

"To prove I'm bad luck," Billy said, "I'd need to trigger a chain reaction of five—to be exact—malfunctions." He counted down on his other hand.

"Five! Betty's cat feeder was on an unstable table. If I bumped into it, the kibble bucket would tip over early, launching the eight ball from the track into...

Four! A sock from Oliver's sock sorter. The robotic arm couldn't handle the impact, so it would fly off and hit...

Three! The pan handle of Christina's breakfast machine. Knowing Christina, she'd jump out of the way to avoid getting egg in her hair, but she'd bump into...

Two! The reverse lever on David and Justin's prankster project. I'm sure David never tested it going backwards, but...

One! I bet he'll wish he could take his words back."
He laughed. "It must be true. I'm 'Bad Luck Billy.'"

The room tilted. Massive tentacles burst through the window.

"Billy, snap out of it. Grab the steering wheel!"
Mister Moonfeld commanded. "We are under attack!"

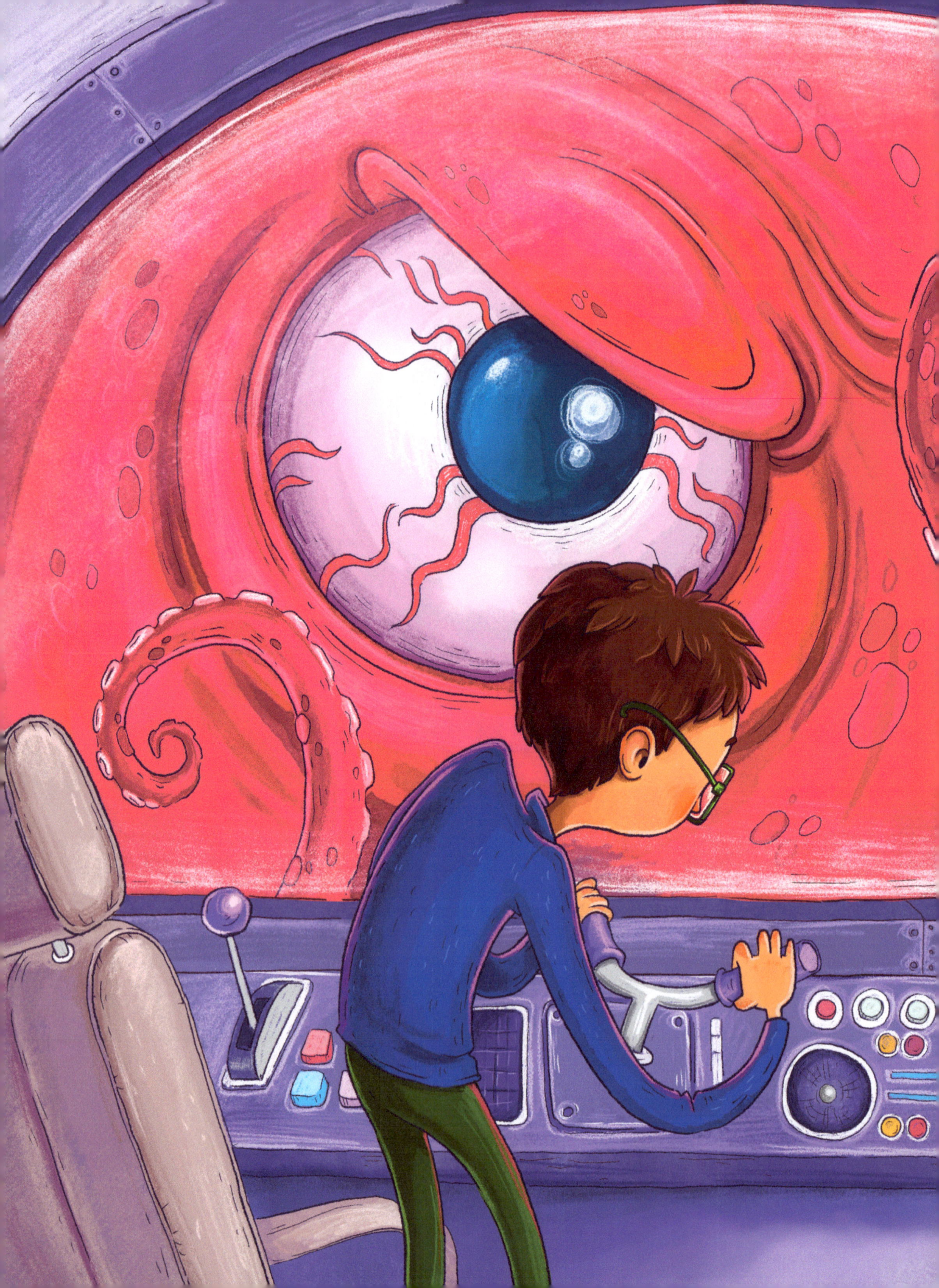

A giant squid coiled around the submarine, squeezing with crushing force.

Billy turned the wheel hard to the right.

The submarine spun free from the squid's grip. The creature released a cloud of black ink before vanishing.

Billy kept his eyes on the control panel, doing his best not to look at the darkness outside. "Can we go now?" he asked.

"We will wait until this ink passes," Mister Moonfeld replied. "Otherwise, who knows where we might end up? That was an incredibly lucky maneuver you pulled."

"It wasn't luck. I don't have any of that," Billy said. "I knew if we went the opposite direction, the squid's elastic tentacles would snap us right back. Spinning was our only escape."

Mister Moonfeld nodded, a carefree smile lighting up his face. "Brilliant, Billy!"

"How come nothing bothers you?" Billy asked, confused. "I'm held down by gravity. You float above the clouds."

The old man chuckled. "Only when I wear my spacesuit. You should try it sometime. I have a spare."

Billy looked up at the swirls of ink.

"Even though the squid is gone, painful feelings linger like this ink," Mister Moonfeld said. "We all have to sit in squid ink at times. It is heavy and dark, but we breathe through it and watch it pass."

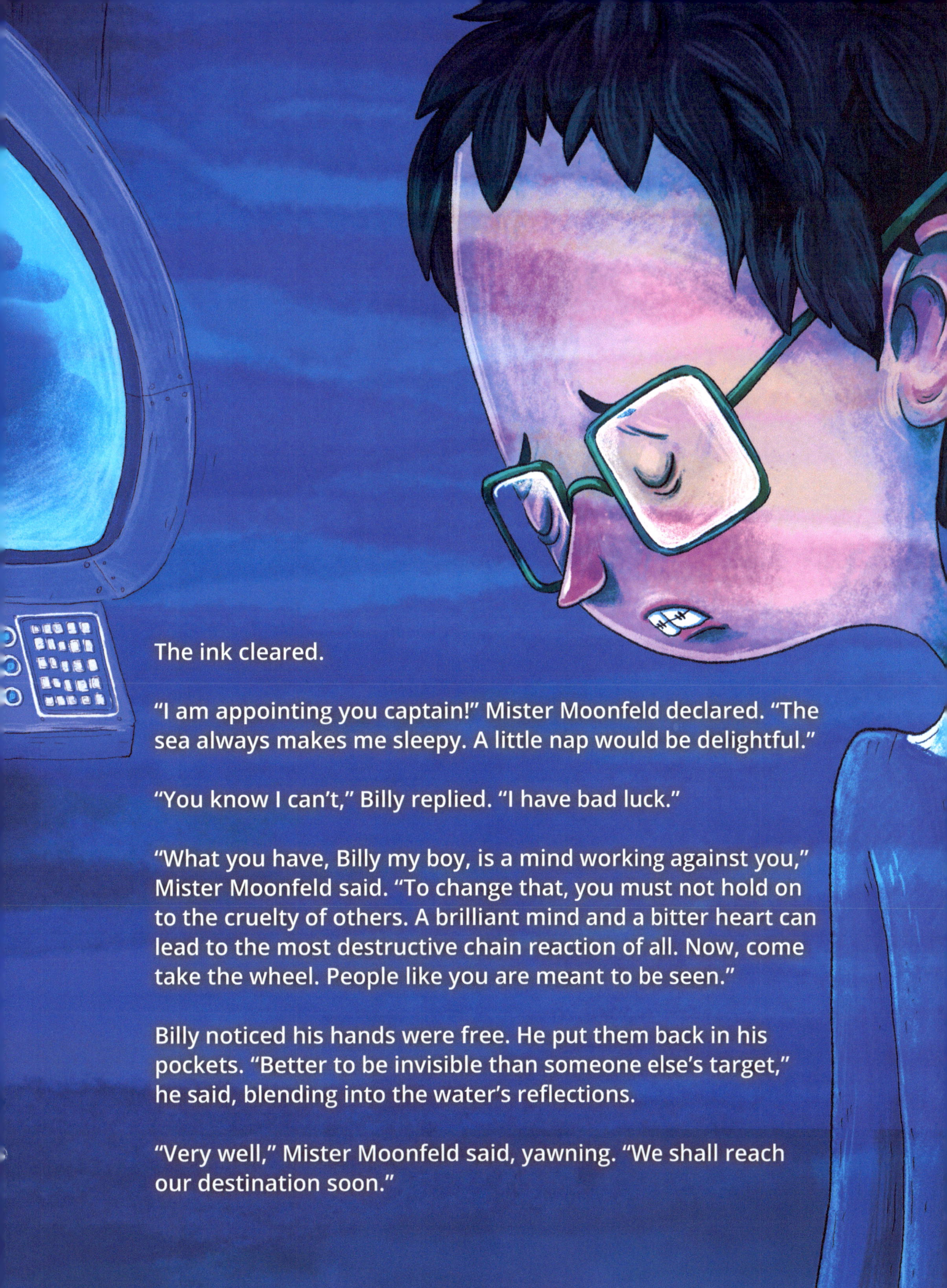

The ink cleared.

"I am appointing you captain!" Mister Moonfeld declared. "The sea always makes me sleepy. A little nap would be delightful."

"You know I can't," Billy replied. "I have bad luck."

"What you have, Billy my boy, is a mind working against you," Mister Moonfeld said. "To change that, you must not hold on to the cruelty of others. A brilliant mind and a bitter heart can lead to the most destructive chain reaction of all. Now, come take the wheel. People like you are meant to be seen."

Billy noticed his hands were free. He put them back in his pockets. "Better to be invisible than someone else's target," he said, blending into the water's reflections.

"Very well," Mister Moonfeld said, yawning. "We shall reach our destination soon."

The engine's steady rhythm filled the cabin.
Billy sat away from the captain's chair, flipping
through the submarine's operation manual.

"Do you know how many controls this
submarine has?" Billy asked, still reading.
"Eighty-four—to be exact."

Billy glanced up from the manual.
Mister Moonfeld was fast asleep,
and they were on a collision course
with a colossal shell!

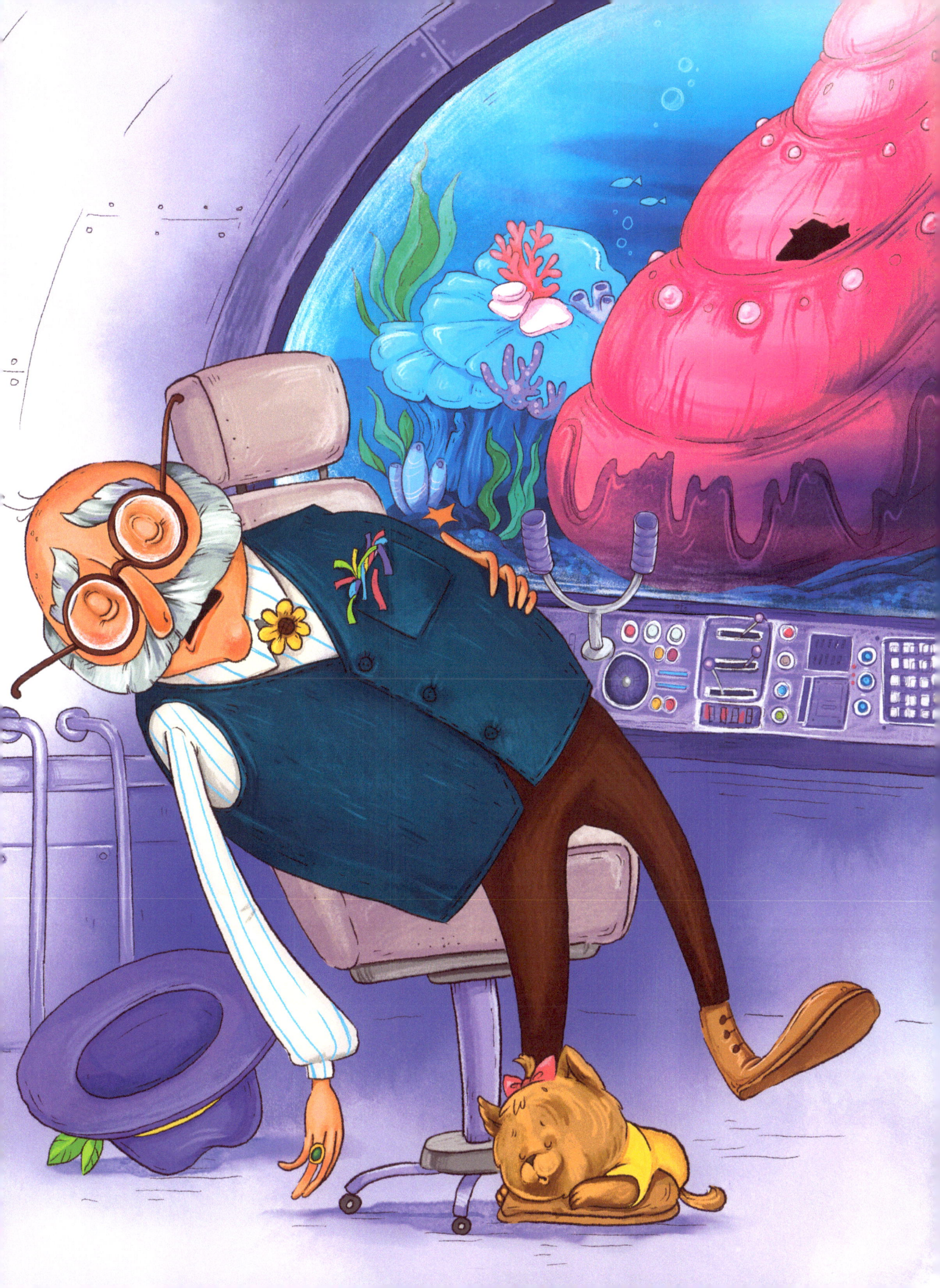

Without a second to spare, Billy gripped the wheel and steered the submarine toward a narrow opening in the shell.

Mister Moonfeld awoke with a snort. "Oh my cosmos!"

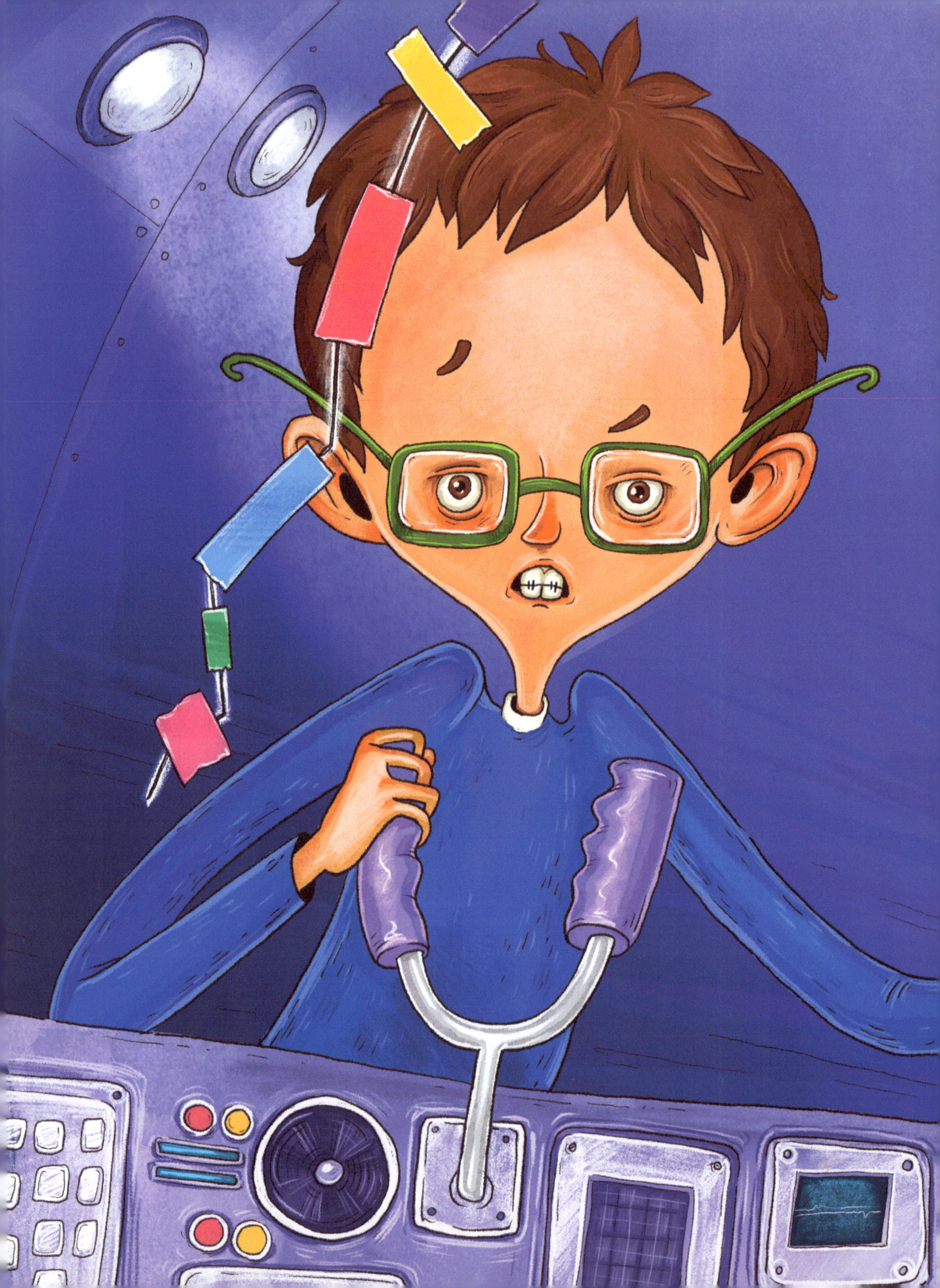

Billy pressed a panel of buttons with one hand and pulled a lever with the other. The machinery hummed to life, propelling them forward through the shell's spiraling tunnel.

"Do you know how many times someone has made fun of my braces?" Billy asked, his words rising like bubbles rushing to the surface. "Sixty-seven—to be exact!"

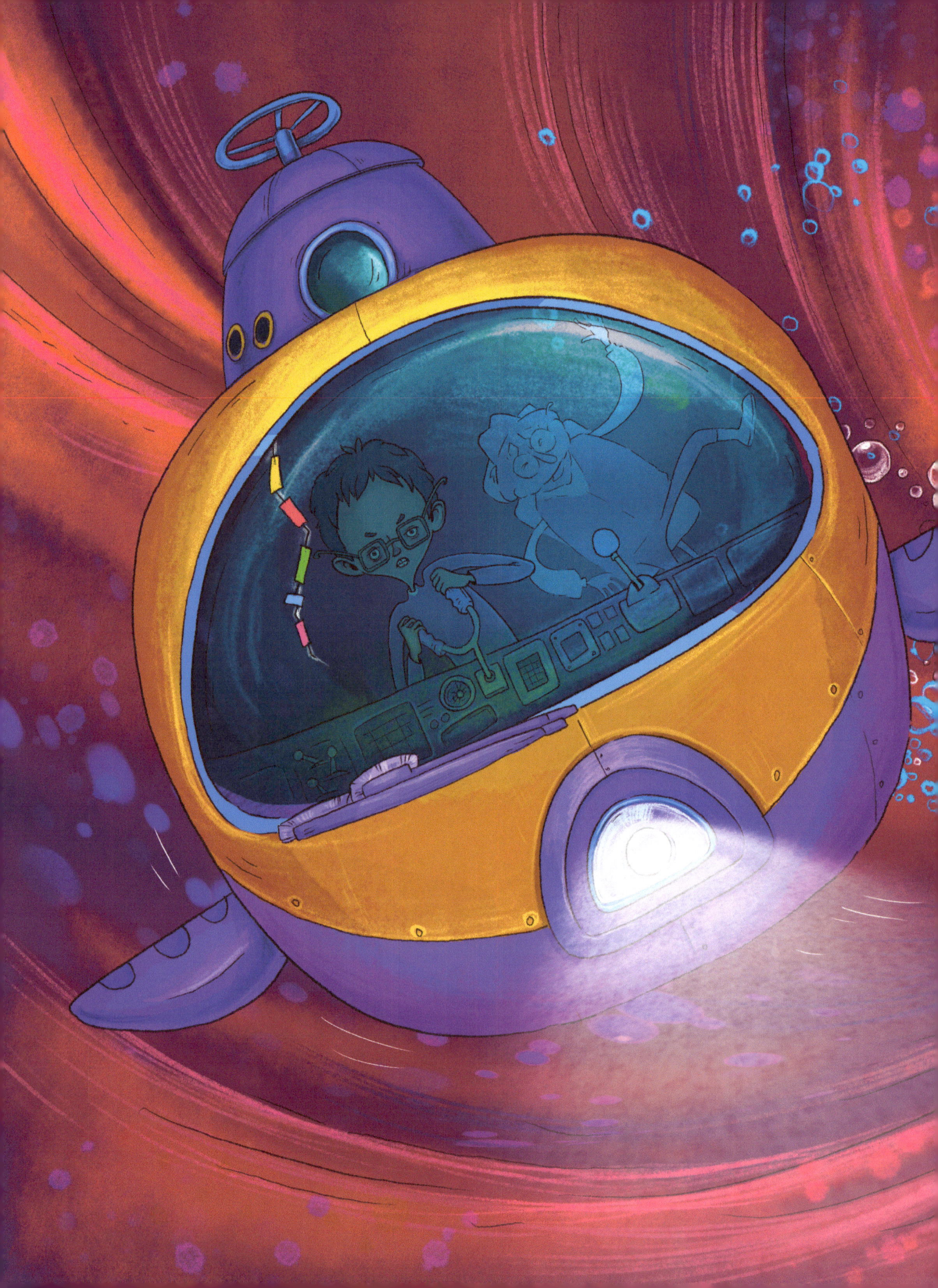

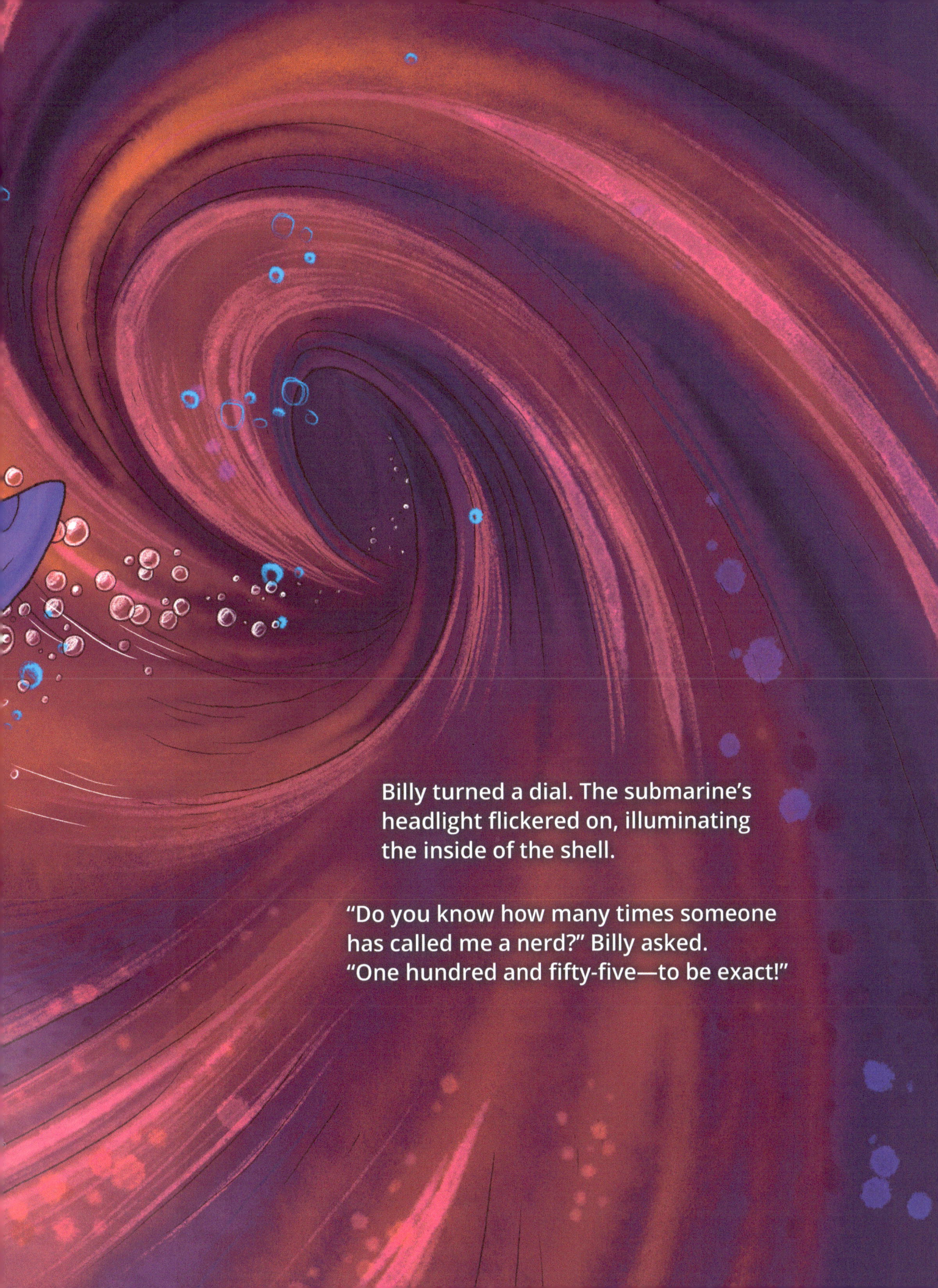

Billy turned a dial. The submarine's headlight flickered on, illuminating the inside of the shell.

"Do you know how many times someone has called me a nerd?" Billy asked.
"One hundred and fifty-five—to be exact!"

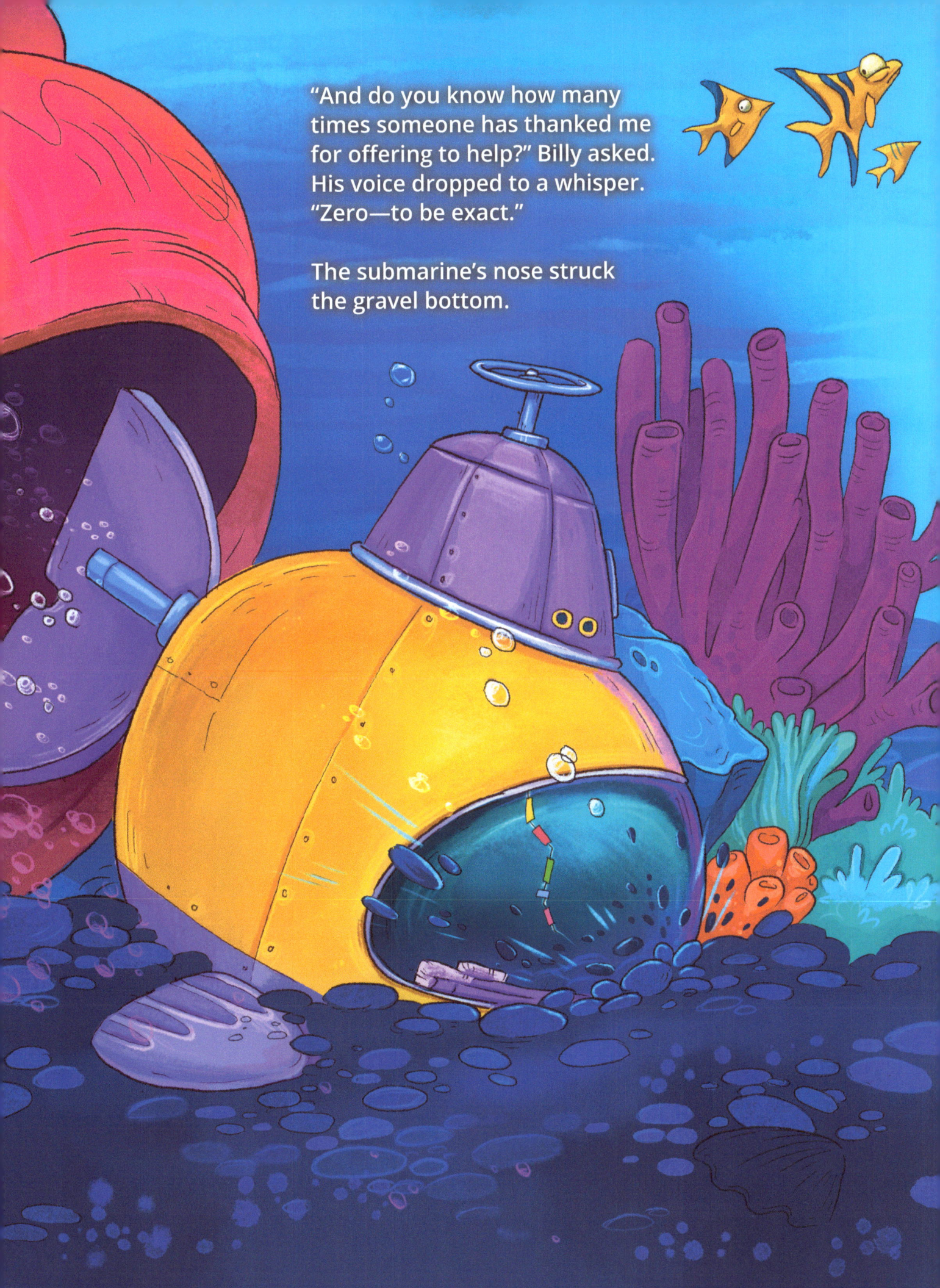

"And do you know how many times someone has thanked me for offering to help?" Billy asked. His voice dropped to a whisper. "Zero—to be exact."

The submarine's nose struck the gravel bottom.

"I always laughed along with them. When I did, it felt like they weren't talking about me. But they were," Billy admitted. "They were always talking about me."

Billy switched on the wipers. "I don't find it funny anymore. They were being mean, and I don't want to be like them. We engineers, we solve problems. We don't make them bigger."

"Absolutely brilliant, Billy," Mister Moonfeld said.

Mister Moonfeld's voice crackled through Billy's headset. "Billy, the way you handled this vessel, you must be the luckiest person I have ever known!"

"There's no such thing as luck," Billy replied. "I read the submarine's manual while you were sleeping."

"If not luck," Mister Moonfeld said, "then what is inside your chest?"

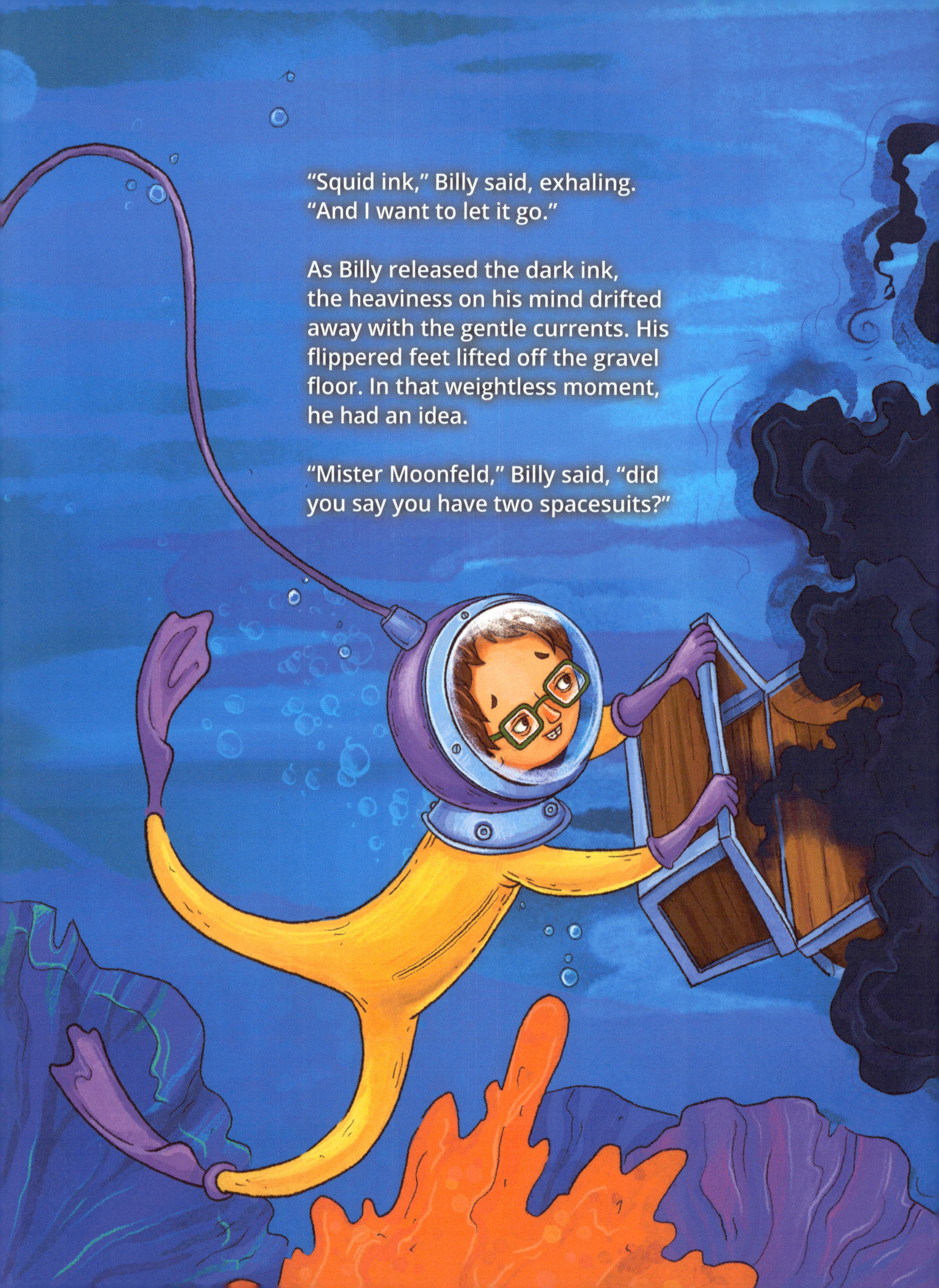

"Squid ink," Billy said, exhaling. "And I want to let it go."

As Billy released the dark ink, the heaviness on his mind drifted away with the gentle currents. His flippered feet lifted off the gravel floor. In that weightless moment, he had an idea.

"Mister Moonfeld," Billy said, "did you say you have two spacesuits?"

Later That Day

"This is awesome!" Billy said,
flying high above the school.

"Billy, I...um...I forgot to tie us down with a rope," Mister Moonfeld said.
"I have no idea how to get us back to the ground."

"I'll figure it out." Billy spread his arms wide. "I have an engineer's mind."

"Brilliant, Billy! Good thing one of us does," Mister Moonfeld said.
"Thank you very much."

Billy smiled and simply replied, "You're welcome."

Thank you for reading!

My greatest wish is to empower the spark in people, young and old, who are passionate about creating a brighter future while having lots of fun along the way!

Until our next journey,

Mister Moonfeld

If you enjoyed this story, please share a smile with someone. If you would like to help others discover it, a review would be wonderful.

MisterMoonfeld.com/review

Continue the adventure...

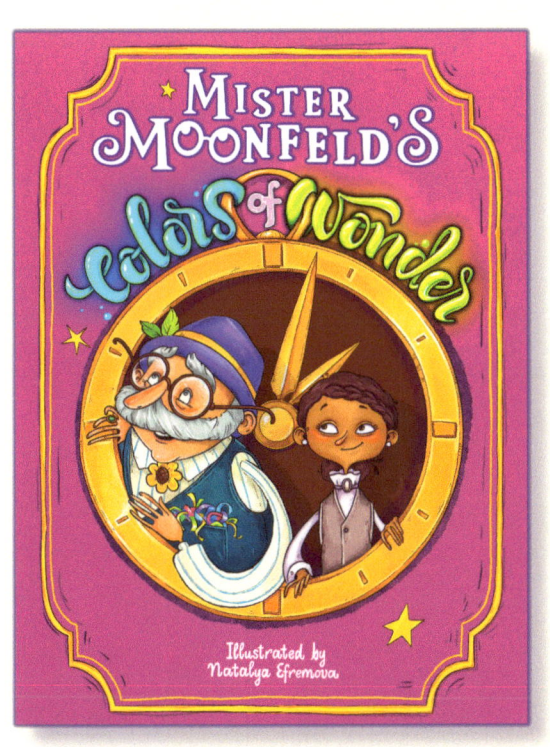

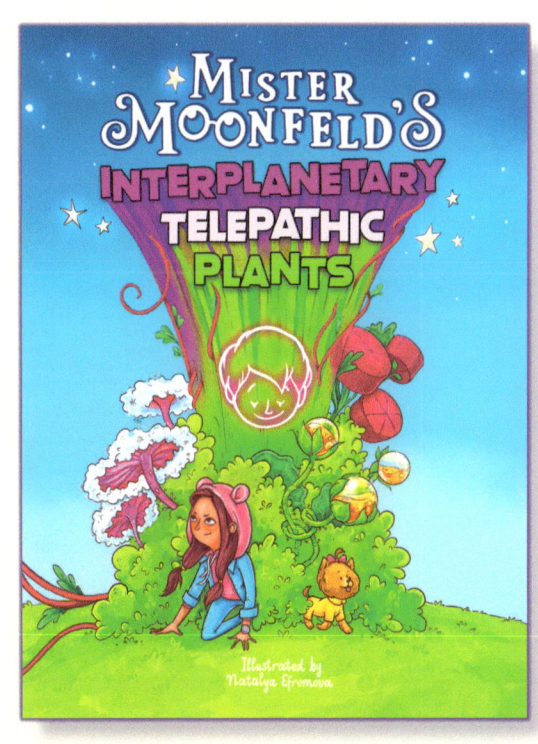